PROJECT
SAFE CHILD

Jeremy's
DECISION

by
ARDYTH BROTT

illustrated by
MICHAEL MARTCHENKO

A CRANKY NELL BOOK

 Kane/Miller Book Publishers
Brooklyn, New York & La Jolla, California

First American paperback edition, 1996

First American Edition 1990 by Kane/Miller Book Publishers
Brooklyn, New York & La Jolla, California

Originally published in Canada in 1990 by Oxford University Press
Text copyright © Ardyth Brott 1990
Illustrations copyright © Michael Martchenko 1990

All rights reserved. For information contact:
Kane/Miller Book Publishers
P.O. Box 310529, Brooklyn, N.Y. 11231-0529

Library of Congress Catalog Card Number 90-61516
ISBN 0-916291-31-6 (hc)
ISBN 0-916291-65-0 (pbk)

Printed and bound in Singapore by Tien Wah Press Pte. Ltd.

1 2 3 4 5 6 7 8 9 10

To
Alexandra, David and Benjamin
— A.B.

To Holly
— M.M.

Jeremy's family was getting ready for the concert. His mother was doing up her black and white dress. His father was putting on his cummerbund and his good cufflinks. His sister, Allegra, was slipping into her shiny black shoes. Jeremy combed his hair and tucked his favourite dinosaur book into his pocket.

Jeremy's family often went to concerts because Mr. Brodski was a conductor. Everyone was happy and excited. Everyone except Jeremy.

It wasn't that Jeremy didn't like music. He did. It wasn't that he minded staying up late. He liked that too. It wasn't that he was tired of watching his father conduct. He loved his father and he loved the concerts.

But people were always asking Jeremy the same question and that question didn't seem to have an answer. Jeremy knew someone would ask it again tonight — at least three times — in front of his father. That was the worst part.

As it happened, Jeremy was right.

They weren't even inside the concert hall before the doorman smiled at Jeremy and asked, "Well, young man, do you think you'll be a conductor like your father?"

It was going to be a long night.

Jeremy didn't want to disappoint his father, but he wasn't ready to make such a big decision. He could feel his ears turn red. "I don't know," he said quietly as he pretended to look at something stuck to the bottom of his shoe.

Jeremy's father brought the orchestra to life. He waved his arms and the violins sang. He pointed his baton and the kettledrums rumbled. He nodded his head and the flutes tootled and trilled.

Jeremy began to feel better. Maybe no one would ask the question again that night. He opened his book and while he read, he noticed how well the melody went with the story. When the music thundered, he could almost see giant dinosaurs fighting. When it was happy, he imagined dinosaurs playing at the edge of a lake. And when it was sad, he watched as the last of the dinosaurs disappeared forever.

The lady sitting beside Jeremy was enjoying herself too. She studied Maestro Brodski through tiny binoculars. Jeremy was so proud he forgot all about the question with no answer. "That's my father," he told her. Right away he was sorry.

"Wonderful!" she whispered. "Are you going to be a conductor too, just like your daddy?"

Quickly, Jeremy looked down at his book. "I don't know," he mumbled.

When the concert was over, everyone began to applaud, but Jeremy clapped the loudest. His father took three bows before the cheering ended.

The three Brodskis hurried backstage to the dressing room. Maestro Brodski was smiling. "Did you like the concert?" he asked.

"I liked the cellos and double basses," said Jeremy. "They made me think of dinosaurs walking in the forest."

"I liked the flutes. They made me think of birds flying through the air," added Allegra.

"I liked the whole thing," Mother said as she gave Father a great big hug.

There was a sharp knock as the door opened. A very fat man with a hat and silver cane entered. "Bravo!" he exclaimed. "Wonderful performance!" He shook Maestro Brodski's hand and kissed Jeremy's mother.

"Dr. Grossenheimer, have you met Allegra and Jeremy? Children, this is Dr. Grossenheimer," said Jeremy's mother.

Dr. Grossenheimer peered down over the rims of his glasses. Then his eyes settled on Jeremy. Before he spoke, Jeremy knew what was coming.

"Tell me, young man, are you going to be a famous musician like your father?"

Poor Jeremy. For the third time that night he replied, "I don't know," as he busied himself picking imaginary fluff from the front of his jacket.

A lady in a long gown and a huge strand of pearls came in next. She wore sparkling silver shoes and long red gloves. She was the Duchess of Ramsbottom.

"So this is your little son," she cried. Jeremy blushed as she kissed the top of his head and squeezed his face so that he looked like a fish.

"Tell me, young man, are you going to be a conductor like your father?"

Four times in one night! Jeremy wanted to run, but everyone was looking at him. "I do not know, madam," he said as politely as he could. Then he began to scratch at a mosquito bite that had just appeared on his hand.

Jeremy didn't want to meet anyone else. He went to a corner and buried his nose in his book.

Just then a man came to interview Maestro Brodski. He carried a notebook and pencil and had a camera slung over his shoulder. "Mischa," he cried. "Congratulations! I've never heard the orchestra sound so beautiful."

Jeremy's father smiled. "Thank you, Gordon. Do you remember our children, Allegra and Jeremy?"

Allegra smiled shyly but Jeremy pretended not to hear. He stared even more closely at his book. The man walked over to Jeremy and stood in front of him. Jeremy held his breath.

Gordon bent close to Jeremy and smiled into his face. Then he looked down at the book and read the title.

"Jeremy," he said, "are you interested in dinosaurs?"

Jeremy couldn't believe his ears. "Why yes I am. Are you, sir?"

"Of course! I think dinosaurs are terrific. Which one is your favourite?"

"The Stegosaurus," said Jeremy. "He didn't eat other dinosaurs. He was a plant eater. He had four long spikes on his tail for protection, and bony plates on his back that the sun would heat up to help him keep warm. He lived about a hundred and sixty million years ago. I saw one in a museum once — at least the bones, and . . ."

He stopped and took a deep breath. Gordon had listened to every word.

And then it happened. Jeremy made his decision.

"You see," Jeremy said, "what I'd really like to do is go and dig up dinosaur bones and study them and learn more about them. I'm going to be a paleontologist when I grow up, **NOT** a conductor."

The dressing room became very quiet. The Duchess of Ramsbottom gasped and pursed her lips so that *she* looked like a fish. Dr. Grossenheimer coughed and peered through his little glasses. He looked very stern and a little like a bullfrog. Even Allegra stared at Jeremy with a surprised look on her face.

Finally Jeremy looked at his parents. Both of them were smiling.

"Bravo!" shouted Jeremy's father.

"I knew it all along," claimed his mother.

"Good lad," sputtered Dr. Grossenheimer.

"Clever boy!" cried the Duchess of Ramsbottom.

Jeremy was so happy, he said it again, just to hear the sound of it. "My father is a conductor, but I am going to be a paleontologist."

"Good for you," said Gordon Alexander.

And Allegra simply smiled.

So years later, if you went to the mountains, you might find Jeremy listening to music as he dug for bones and imagined dinosaurs playing at the edge of a lake.

And ...

... if you hurried back to the city, you might get there just in time to see Allegra, dressed in her shiny black shoes, taking her final bow.